Harry
the
Hairy-Nosed Wombat

& other
Australian Animal Tales

Jill Morris

illustrated by Tina Wilson

published by Greater Glider Productions
Queensland Australia
www.greaterglider.com

For this anthology Jill Morris has rewritten six of her favourite stories based on Australian wildlife, which were first published in 1970-2 by Golden Press.

illustrated by Tina Wilson
edited by Cheryl Wickes
typeset by Range Rose
printed by Fergies, Hamilton Queensland
bound by Special Equipment, Hemmant Queensland

published by Greater Glider Productions
BOOK FARM 8 Rees Lane Maleny
Queensland 4552 Australia

Cataloguing-in-Publication data
        Morris, Jill, 1936- .
        Harry the hairy-nosed wombat & other Australian animal tales.

        For children
        ISBN 0 947304 67 3.

        I. Animals - Juvenile fiction. 2. Children's stories, Australian
        I. Wilson, Tina. II. Title. III. Title : Harry the hairy-nosed wombat
        and other Australian animal tales.

A823.3

Australian Animal Tales

Harry the Hairy-Nosed Wombat

arry came out of his burrow, nose up, sniffing the air. His whiskers bristled, and the hairs on his large nose quivered. He couldn't see very well, but he had a very good sense of smell and his pointed ears could pick up the slightest sound.

It was dark, and the air above the burrow was cool. In the daytime the sun beat down on the dry land.

In their tunnels under the rocks, the wombats could escape the heat of the day. Now that night had come, it was time for wombats to waddle out and feed.

Harry's feeding ground was a patch of grass under a saltbush. Harry had worn a little track to it over the dry ground. Sometimes he nibbled the leaves of the saltbush or dug up little balls of fungus that popped out of the sandy soil. Past Harry's feeding ground was the sea, where waves licked the sand along a white beach.

Harry was a hairy-nosed wombat. His nose was covered in soft, silky hair. His teeth were long and sharp for chewing. His fur was dark grey and full of dust from digging. His sharp claws were like small black shovels. Most of all, Harry liked digging and chewing.

When Harry was a baby he had lived in his mother's pouch until he had fur all over his body and he was big enough to explore the world outside. Later he had dug his own burrow, where he could live alone.

The colony of hairy-nosed wombats all had tunnels under limestone rocks, which hid the entrance holes from view.

One day several large trucks moved along the dirt track near Harry's burrow and stopped. The men in the trucks had been sent to turn the dirt track into a bitumen highway. The limestone rocks were in the way.

All day bulldozers bit and tore into the earth, pushing the stones into huge piles. Graders pushed the soil down flat. When Harry came out of his hole that night, the machines looked like black monsters waiting to pounce.

When he went to his feeding ground, he saw men standing on the beach. He turned and lumbered back to his hole.

The new road was to go right through the pile of rocks that hid Harry's burrow. Every day, when Harry was trying to sleep, bulldozers nosed their way through the hard soil. The noise was deafening. The ground shook and shivered. Harry dug deeper into the floor of his burrow and put his head down as low as he could.

When he woke up for his evening meal, the noise had stopped. Time to get up. He was hungry. He moved sleepily along his tunnel. Soil and stones had fallen from the roof into an untidy pile on the floor. He raked them aside with his claws. Then he stopped. A boulder was blocking the exit to his burrow.

'HUMPH!' grunted Harry. No boulder would stop him. He lay on his side and tore at the soil around the boulder with his front claws. Then he pushed the soil with his front legs, right through under his body. His back legs kicked it out of the way.

At last, with a snort, he clambered out into the clear night air, shook the dust from his fur, and followed the path to his feeding ground.

When he had finished eating, he squeezed back into his tunnel through the new entrance. After a long night of hard work, he curled up and went to sleep.

Early in the morning, when the men came back to start work, they found Harry's tracks across the new road and the huge, gaping hole. They started up their engines. AARGH! BUMP! The bulldozers filled in the hole.

By nightfall the road was nearly finished. Harry woke up hungry, found his exit blocked again, lay on his side and began to dig. At last he stood under the evening sky and lumbered off to his feeding ground.

When the men saw the hole was there again, back came the bulldozers to fill it in.

What sort of animal could be making these holes? the men wondered. They looked down into the tunnel to find out where it led, but it was too dark to see anything.

One man tried to investigate and became stuck, upside down, and had to be pulled out by the feet.

'These holes are everywhere,' said one of the roadworkers. 'They must all connect together and meet underground.'

'Wombats!' said Fred the foreman. 'We're doing battle with wombats.'

That night, when Harry poked his nose out into the fresh air, Fred was waiting. 'A wombat!' he said. 'I told you so. But it's not an ordinary wombat. See his hairy nose?'

'He looks like a pig,' said one of the men.

'Or a badger.'

'Or a bear.'

Fred looked at Harry. 'So you're the fellow who's been causing all the trouble.'

Harry lifted his front leg and, reaching along as far as he could, scratched his back. Then he HUMPH-ed back into his burrow.

Next day Harry had his best sleep in weeks. No work was done on the road. Big black cars brought very important people in dark suits, who paced up and down the road near Harry's home. They followed his path and found a patch of grass under a saltbush and puffy balls of fungus that popped out of the sandy soil. They found little piles of square wombats' droppings.

Soon the dark suits were as dusty as wombats' fur.

'It's very clever,' said one, 'the way these wombats dig tunnels.'

'You know,' said another, 'wombats are fine engineers.'

Standing near Harry's burrow, they made a decision. 'Let's take the road around the rocks. There'll be an extra curve, but what does it matter in all these miles?'

Soon the bulldozer, the grader, all the roadworkers and Fred the foreman went home, leaving a black ribbon of highway with a curve around a clump of limestone rocks.

Underneath the rocks, in his underground home, Harry slept. He had earned a rest.

This was the place he liked best. There were tufts of grass only a wombat-walk away, and puffy balls of fungus if you knew where to look and had sharp claws for digging. And roots underground, if you had sharp teeth for chewing. And sandhills, where waves licked the sand along a white beach.

A dry land – but the perfect place to live if you happened to be a hairy-nosed wombat.

Wombats are found only in Australia. The Common Wombat is found in Tasmania, Victoria and New South Wales. Harry, the hero of this story, is a Southern Hairy-nosed Wombat, a species found in South Australia. A third species, the Northern Hairy-nosed Wombat, living in only one area in Queensland, is endangered.

Rufus the Red Kangaroo

ufus hopped as quickly as he could across the dry, red earth and jumped head-first into his mother's pouch.

His mother tried to push him out, but Rufus wanted to stay in the pouch as long as he could.

Whenever he jumped into the pouch, his head went in first, while his legs poked out behind him. His body wriggled around inside to make room for his legs, then his head popped out and off he went riding, wherever his mother carried him.

Today the legs wouldn't fit. Rufus's head was in the pouch, but there was no space to turn around. His mother pushed with her paws, telling him to climb out. He was too big!

Rufus didn't want to come out. He twisted and squirmed, wriggled with his body and kicked with his legs, but it was no use. Out he came backwards, until he stood facing his mother.

Rufus was a red kangaroo, with rusty-red fur all over his body. His front legs barely touched the ground as he moved along slowly, eating grass. His strong back legs gave him speed while hopping and his long tail gave him balance.

Rufus's father was a Big Red Kangaroo. One day soon Rufus would be a Big Red too.

It was so hot and dry where Rufus lived that only the toughest animals could survive. Snakes and lizards of many kinds lived under rocks, and most of them were camouflaged the same colour as the ground.

As Rufus watched, a Thorny Devil came out into the sun. Although he was very small, Thorny looked like a dinosaur. All along his back the skin rose in lumps, each topped by a prickly spike. Above his eyes were two fierce horns. In the glare of the sun the tough, dark grey skin turned to the reddish-brown of the ground.

Thorny moved very slowly. He had no need to run. There was not a spot on that back where an enemy could bite without taking a mouthful of prickles. Thorny stored moisture under his skin and could go without water for a very long time.

Rufus was curious about the strange little lizard, but he was afraid to poke his soft nose too close to those spikes.

He lifted his head and sniffed the hot, dry air. The land was baked in crusts and cracked in lines after months without rain. There was no fresh, green grass. For kangaroos there was no food.

During the day when the sun was hot, Rufus and the other kangaroos rested in the shade of the mulga trees. At dusk they searched for food. But grass was becoming harder to find. Most of the clumps had been nibbled to the roots. Rivers had turned into lines of cracked holes. Lakes had turned into beds of salt.

The kangaroos would die unless they could find food.

Wherever Rufus went, the Rock was always near. It stood alone on the plain, yet it seemed to be lying down like a crouching dingo ready to spring.

High in the Rock were caves, where hunters long ago had painted pictures of kangaroos and lizards in the colours of the earth: yellow, creamy-white and the red of Rufus's fur.

Rufus waited with the other kangaroos until the sun had almost disappeared. As the mob moved off to find food, the leaders went first. From far away they had picked up the scent of water. They would follow it to find moisture and food.

Rufus and the other young kangaroos had to keep up. Small joeys travelled in the pouch – they would have an easy ride. Dust rose in a cloud as the mob thundered over the dry earth.

The leaders were moving very fast. Rufus was taking his longest jumps but he was being left behind. Red dust swirled through the rays of the afternoon sun, more dust than the mob could raise. They had been caught in a dust storm.

Rufus couldn't see. The smell of the dust blocked out the scent of the other kangaroos. His ears turned as he strained to hear some sound that would tell him the way to go.

Then he heard a faint BOOM-BOOM-BOOM! He hopped off quickly, following the sound.

At last, through the dust, he saw his mother and father and the rest of the mob. They were resting among trees in the shelter of a clump of rocks.

BOOM-BOOM-BOOM! Rufus almost flew across the ground. At last he stood among them, tired out from his journey. Then he noticed they were drinking water and eating grass. He joined them, lapping the water with his tongue and chewing fresh blades of green.

The next day, all the grass was gone. The mob rested under the trees. At nightfall they would move back towards the Rock.

By afternoon black clouds had gathered overhead. Rufus sniffed moisture on the air. Under the palm trees, a frog croaked.

The kangaroos were off, the leaders in a bunch. The rest of the pack followed. Rufus set off, his tail high in the air. BOOM-BOOM-BOOM!

Then another booming noise was heard. BOOM! CRACK! The clouds were talking to one another. The sun had gone, leaving the storm to battle on alone.

Rufus hopped along with the pack. Lightning came, and thunder. Rufus kept hopping. Rain started to fall. His fur stood up in patches and rivers of water cascaded down his back. But he kept up with the mob and this time he did not lose his way.

All through the night rain fell, cascading down the Rock wherever it could find a path. Rufus sheltered beneath the mulgas with the other kangaroos. The air was cool. Mud squelched between his claws.

When the rain stopped, the Rock shone in the morning sun. It wasn't red at all, but pink and grey, with streaks of cream. The heads of the round mountains in the distance looked as if they had been scrubbed.

A rainbow curved across the sky.

Rufus fluffed his fur out to dry and flicked the mud from the end of his tail.

The mother kangaroos turned their joeys out and licked their pouches clean.

Birds appeared – white parrots, budgerigars, pink brolgas and pelicans with wings spread wide. Wild geese honked as they flew.

The land was not dead and dry. It had been resting, waiting for rain.

Soon Rufus would be standing in waving grass in the shade of the mulgas. He would have to be strong to survive as a Big Red, but he was part of this land.

Bobuck the Mountain Possum

obuck skidded along the branch, tail flying. A monster had just arrived under his tree. He scrambled back to watch from the safety of his mother's back.

Bobuck had never seen one of these monsters before. His mother knew it was a car, but cars meant campers, and campers meant noise in the daytime when possums like to sleep, and dangers at night when possums like to hunt.

Bobuck's mother had never been harmed by people. As more of the monsters arrived, she told Bobuck not to be afraid.

While the possums watched, the people unpacked their cars. They put up tents. They set up a kitchen under a tree, where the food would be shaded during the day. They brought pillows and blankets, unfolded stretchers and spread out sleeping bags.

Bobuck's home was a hole in the hollow of a large tree which stood on a patch of grass beside the creek. On the other side, the bank rose to a steep cliff. In paddocks up above, cows grazed. Above the paddocks towered a mountain.

In some places the mountain was covered with trees. In others, smooth cliff faces rose steep and dangerous.

Bobuck belonged to a family of possums that live in mountainous areas of eastern Australia. His fur was dark grey, nearly black, with white underneath his body. He had large black eyes, short ears and a pink nose. His tail was thick and bushy. On the underside of his tail was a strip of rough skin for gripping the bark of trees.

When Bobuck was very small he had spent six weeks in his mother's pouch until his body was covered in fur and he was strong enough to ride like a jockey on her back.

If the possums heard a noise, which meant danger might be near, his mother stood up on her back legs, front paws held up and ready to fight. Her black eyes glared a warning and she made her fighting call: UH-UH-UH! like breathing grunts.

At night Bobuck and his mother came down out of their tree to hunt for fern fronds, insects, nectar from flowering trees and fruit. Sometimes as she passed a fallen log, Bobuck's mother would stop, sniff the air, then rub her furry chest against the rough bark.

'I'm leaving our special smell behind,' she said. 'The next mountain possum to come along will know that we have been here and will rub in the same spot.'

'Can I do it too?' When Bobuck rubbed his chest against the bark of the log, it tickled!

The people camping beneath the tree woke early in the morning. They collected wood for the fire and cooked their breakfast over red hot coals. They washed their faces in the creek, leaning out over the water to see their reflections. They dug up clay and painted pictures on the rocks.

At night, while the billy boiled, they sat around the fire and sang to the strumming of an old guitar. They played tunes on gum leaves and banged saucepan lids together. They watched the moon rise in the sky like a giant yellow ball. As Bobuck and his mother came down the tree for their nightly hunt, the children were eating apples.

The smallest child put a half-eaten apple on the ground and watched to see what the possums would do.

Bobuck's mother pushed him off her back and skidded down the tree. She grasped the apple in her front paws and shot back up to where Bobuck was waiting. Bobuck held the apple in his front paws and bit into the white flesh, while the children cheered.

Next morning two of the men from the camp set off to climb the mountain, a dark silhouette against the sun.

The children spent the day playing in the paddock and exploring along the creek.

When night came, Bobuck was waiting for the children to bring him another apple. But a large group of people had gathered under the tree. The men who had set off to climb the mountain had not returned.

The possums, camouflaged in the branches above, went back to hide in their hole. There would be no apples.

All night the lights of the search party twinkled on the mountain while a giant moon hung in the sky.

In the morning the men were still missing. All day helicopters buzzed around the mountain. THUNK-THUNK-THUNK!

'Where's Brian? Bri-an!' Now one of the children was missing! A young boy had gone walking up the creek, looking for his father.

There would be no apples that night. Bobuck and his mother scuttled down the tree hidden by shadows, and went off into the darkness to hunt. They crossed the creek by their own little bridge, a fallen log.

Bobuck was riding on his mother's back. Suddenly she stopped, back straight and body held upright. Bobuck almost fell off. His mother lifted her front paws and made her special fighting call: UH-UH-UH! like breathing grunts.

In front of them stood a boy. It was Brian and he was lost. He was trying not to be afraid. He had crossed the creek in the afternoon, heading up the hill. He had seen a helicopter whirling like a giant bird. Then it had grown dark. Now he was lost and alone.

Brian recognised Bobuck's face peering over his mother's shoulder. He wished the possums could show him the way back to camp.

Bobuck's mother turned and scampered lightly back across the fallen log, then turned and stood very still on the other side of the creek, watching the boy.

Brian thought, 'If the possums can go that way, perhaps I can too.'

He put one foot on the log and felt it sway under his weight. But he knew he must try. Carefully, one foot after the other, Brian stepped out across the log. It was so dark he could hardly see where to place his feet, and the surface was slippery. But once he had started he could not go back.

Just as Brian reached the middle of the log, the full moon rose from behind the mountain and lit up his path like a golden road. He crossed in safety and arrived on the other side.

The possums scampered back to their tree.

Now, with the moon to light his way, the boy easily found the path back to camp. Everyone was relieved to see him safely home. Before he went to bed, Brian left some pieces of apple at the foot of the tree where Bobuck would be able to find them.

Next morning, one of the helicopter pilots saw a flash of colour on a mountain ledge. The searchers sent messages to one another and the men were winched to safety. The search was called off.

At last everyone could go home. Bobuck watched them leave. His little world was quiet again.

'Will the people come back?' he asked his mother.

'They've all gone off to their own homes, but they'll be back. You'll see.'

Bobuck could hardly wait. His bushy tail quivered and his round ears bristled as he asked his mother, 'Will there be apples?'

Kolo the Bush Koala

large old male koala grunted as he peered through the side of the truck at the trees rushing past. Kolo, too, was afraid.

She seemed to have been in the truck for a very long time. The gum leaves had withered and they no longer tasted juicy and sweet.

The koalas made loud wailing sounds like the noise of the wind in the electric wires above their heads. But the truck rumbled on.

When the men had arrived to catch the animals, Kolo had been reaching high to the freshest leaves. The koalas nearest the ground were sleepy and were lifted gently from their perch.

Kolo had seen what was happening and tried to get away.

But one of the men had climbed a long ladder and dropped a loop of rope around her body, then pulled until she lost her balance and fell into the net held by other men below.

Kolo was the last to be caught. She struggled. She scratched with her sharp claws. But she was put into a crate and the door was shut with a CLANG!

There were many other koalas on the truck with her – some sleeping, some squealing, some grunting their annoyance, some nibbling on leaves.

The jolting of the rough road loosened the door of Kolo's cage. When the truck bounced higher than ever, the door swung open and Kolo pushed her way out. The truck was grinding slowly up a hill as she leapt to the ground.

There was a steep drop beside the road and Kolo's furry body rolled over and over, down the slope. Her claws scrabbled for something to break her fall and she grasped a clump of grass that grew above a rock. She clung to the grass. Above was a steep cliff. Below was the water of a very cold lake.

'What are you doing up there?' A voice drifted up to her, carried on the wind.

Below, in a small boat, sat a man in a checked shirt and old trousers, his face hidden behind a beard as grey and grizzly as Kolo's fur.

The man stood up in the boat and reached towards her. 'Steady there, old girl! This water's too cold for a swim.'

Kolo scratched at the reaching hands and the man almost fell out of the boat. He grabbed his fishing net and threw it over her struggling body.

With Kolo trapped in the net, Joe steered across the lake towards the jetty where he moored his boat.

'What were you doing up there?' he asked. 'There are no koalas in these parts any more. They died out years ago when the trees were cleared...

I know! They're bringing koalas from places where the food's running out, to be re-located to the island in the lake. Plenty of food there for you – the gum trees you love, and other animals – emus, wallabies. This afternoon I'll take you to the Rangers' office. They'll know what to do.'

Joe took Kolo to his cottage high above the lake. He trapped her under his laundry basket on the verandah while he ate his lunch. Kolo was waiting for the moment when she could escape again.

The old man pointed towards the lake. 'There's a town down there,' he said, 'under the water. Some of the old houses were flooded when they constructed the dam. Some were moved to higher ground. They brought my house up here on the back of a truck. I know what it's like to have to move from your home.'

The voice grew softer and the creaking of the rocking chair grew slower. The old man was asleep.

Kolo shuffled the basket along the verandah until it tumbled off the edge and she was able to wriggle free and set out through Joe's gate, on to the dusty road.

The sun burned into her fur and her nose felt dry and prickly. She was hungry but there were no trees along the road, only rough, jagged stones that pricked her paws. Her claws skidded on the stones.

The road spread like a brown ribbon in front of her. Rounding a curve, she stopped. In front of her was a truck, like the one she had travelled in that morning. A ramp was propped against its open back.

As Kolo edged around one of the tall black wheels, a speeding car screamed past and sent her scrambling up the ramp. The scraping noise of the ramp being pushed back into the truck made her huddle behind a pile of sacks to hide. The sacks smelled musty but she snuggled into

them and went to sleep. The truck pulled away, leaving tyre marks in the dust. Nearby were the tracks of a young koala.

Joe woke on his verandah in the sleepy afternoon and realised Kolo had gone. He searched the yard, then the road, where he found Kolo's tracks and the tyre marks of the truck. He got out his old car and went off in search of her. If Kolo was on board the truck, she was headed into the mountains where there were no gum trees to eat.

When Kolo woke, the truck had stopped and the driver was walking into a building. She wriggled from the sacks and was halfway to the ground when a large dog bounded across the road.

Kolo galloped off up the hill, with the dog close behind.

The hillside was pitted with deep holes from old mines, marked with DANGER! signs.

Trying to escape from the dog, Kolo slipped under one of the signs and fell into the deep darkness of an old gold mine.

The world tumbled and Kolo's claws scrabbled in mid-air. She landed heavily on a large wooden beam stretching across the mine shaft. A damp, woody smell drifted up to her from below. Above, the shadow of the dog was silhouetted against the sky. The dog was yapping, barking, growling. Kolo clung to the beam and squealed in fright.

'Down, boy!' shouted a voice.

'So there you are, little one!' Joe's familiar voice echoed down the mine. 'In another pretty pickle! Hold on – we'll soon have you out!'

Joe swung his legs over the edge of the shaft and was lowered slowly down on a rope. He gathered Kolo in his arms and signalled for the rope to be pulled up.

When they were safe in the open air above, Joe told Kolo firmly, 'I'm taking you to the island myself.'

'I understand what it's like to be moved,' he told her as he drove back down the mountain in his old car.

'I had no choice when the town was flooded by the lake,' he told her as he placed her firmly in his boat.

'It was harder for me because I was old. You'll start a new life here,' he told her as he lifted her gently into a tree.

As Joe's boat chugged away from the island, he looked back and saw movement in the gums. And above the coughing of his outboard motor he imagined he could hear grunting coughs, the sound of koalas talking to one another.

Kolo is said to be one of the names given to koalas by Australian Aborigines. It means 'no drink'. Koalas do not drink water but obtain enough moisture from dew and gum leaves.

Percy the Peaceful Platypus

That winter, in a quiet corner of Australia, a mother platypus dug a nesting burrow at the end of a tunnel beside a shallow pool.

In that warm, safe place she made a damp nest of grass, leaves and willow-roots.

In the nest she laid two creamy-white leathery eggs that were lightly joined together. She placed them on her broad, flat tail, curled the rest of her body around them, and there she stayed for two weeks, until it was time for her babies to hatch.

Percy was the first. His small, soft head with a rubbery bill pushed its way out of the broken shell. Percy had no fur and he could not see, but he scratched at the shell until he was free.

His mother nudged him gently with her bill then turned to his sister, who was breaking out of the shell beside him.

The baby platypuses had much to learn before they could swim on their own in the pool below.

Percy loved to eat! He was always hungry, and when darkness came he would go on a picnicking swim which lasted all night long. When he was hunting, he closed his eyes and ears and let his rubbery bill lead him to slippery worms which he gobbled by the hundred with a mouthful of mud; and tadpoles, fat and black with wriggling tails.

Ever alert to danger, Percy learned to dive and lie still on the creek bed when anything strange approached his quiet pool.

By the time he was almost fully grown, his upper body was covered in dark brown fur, while the fur underneath was a silvery grey. On each of his four feet, the toes were joined by skin that stretched wide when he was swimming. When he walked on land, the webbing on his front feet was folded back, so he looked as if he might be going backwards.

Percy could swim like a fish, or walk on land like a lizard. He could burrow like a wombat and he had fur like a possum. Yet he had come from an egg!

When it was time for Percy to leave his mother's burrow, he travelled upstream and found the perfect place – the bank of a pool hidden by overhanging trees.

Using his bill as a shovel and his claws as a rake, he made a long tunnel where he could hide from danger, predators and noise. The entrance was just large enough for him to squeeze through.

When the digging was completed, he combed his fur with his claws and went to bed for the day in his new home.

In the daylight silver beetles skimmed the surface of the pool with the power of rockets. Dragonflies lifted their wings and rose in the air with a flurry of blue.

While Percy was asleep in his burrow, Kilai the blue and white crayfish came creeping sideways from under a rock. But when the platypus woke and began poking about with his bill, Kilai sidled back to safety.

One day, Percy's peace was disturbed. Far away, a huge storm was brewing. Satellites in space warned of its coming. In their homes, people watched barometer needles falling. A pattern of wind and rain, whirling in a circle, showed up on radar screens along the coast.

Cyclone Sally was on her way! Whirling in at 160 kilometres an hour, Sally shook houses on their foundations, lifted roofs and sent trees crashing to the ground.

The sea, whipped up by gale-force winds, flung its waves like weapons at the shore. Inland, Percy sensed that something was about to happen and snuggled closer in his hole.

As quickly as she had come, Sally blew herself out to sea. But after her came the flood.

Heavy rain fell in the mountains, swelling the creeks and rushing towards the sea. Percy's little pool turned into a raging torrent. The bank near Percy's burrow cracked under the weight of water and slid into the creek. He was carried out into the flood.

As he tried to swim against the current, he was hit by a floating log and his limp body was carried away downstream.

With the passing of the flood, a dragonfly lay dead in a muddy pool, her wings smashed. Silver beetles lay helpless in a tangle of leaves.

Percy lay where the torrent had carried him, his legs spread out like broken twigs.

Help was on its way for people stranded by the floods.

OPERATION FLOODBOUND, using army 'Ducks' which could travel in water or on land, had begun!

One crew was sent north. They passed some sheep, stranded in a huddle on a piece of high ground. 'Hang on! We'll pick you up on the way back,' shouted Steve, the driver.

The Duck churned on through sodden fields and headed upstream. The huge wheels stopped short of a furry body lying in a puddle.

'Better investigate,' said Steve.

Tom vaulted over the side of the Duck. 'It's alive. It's a cat!' he shouted. 'No, it's a rabbit. It's a… platypus!'

'Ornithorhynchus,' murmured Steve. 'If it's a male, watch out for its poisonous spurs.'

Tom took off his hat and, wrapping it carefully around Percy's legs, he carried the struggling bundle back to the Duck.

'What are we going to do with him?' Steve wondered. 'We're supposed to be looking for people who need help.'

The soldiers decided to find a safe place to leave Percy, so they followed the creek upstream, climbing to higher ground.

Across the flooded paddocks they saw the red roof of a house and people waving.

'How did you know where to find us?' they asked as they climbed on board.

'We were rescuing one of the other residents,' said Steve. 'He's wriggling over there in Tom's hat.'

In a quiet pool where the trees hung low, Tom released Percy, who waddled down the bank and slipped with a PLOP! into the water.

'Back to work,' sighed Tom. 'We'll get this family back to safety, then come back for the sheep.'

Percy was alone in his new pool. Using his bill as a shovel and his claws as a rake, he began to dig his new burrow.

The following year, a farmer took his children to an auction where ex-army vehicles were being sold. They wanted a Duck for moving stock, but they were looking for one particular Duck – and they found it!

'Going, going…' The auctioneer banged down his hammer. '…Gone! Sold to the gentleman in the broad-brimmed hat!'

The children fingered the Duck with pride. Scratched on the metal side was a name: HMAS PLATYPUS.

The amphibious 'Duck' which will run in water or on land is really spelt DUKW, an abbreviation of a longer German name.

Rusty the Nimble Numbat

flock of red and green parrots screeched down over the rocky mountains. CRAH! CRAH! Their colours flashed as they flew in a cloud.

Nothing else stirred on the hill. Most of the animals were asleep in their burrows, hiding from the sun that scorched the hot desert land.

Rusty poked his snout into a tunnel leading to a termite mound and scooped termites into his mouth with his long, sticky tongue. After feeding he stretched out in the sun, then went back to his burrow where he had made a nest of grass and leaves.

Rusty's fur was a brownish red. Across his back, seven white stripes stood out against the darker fur. A long white stripe ran past each eye, with a darker stripe below it. Underneath his body the fur was creamy yellow. Rusty's tail was almost as long as his head and body combined, and when he ran leaping over the red sand he carried it like a banner. When he was feeding it stood high in the air, fluffed up like a bottlebrush.

Many other animals lived on the hill, some of them Rusty's predators: Python, Sand Goanna and Chuditch the Native Cat. With five young cubs to feed, Chuditch was always hunting.

Sometimes Rusty played with Pitchi Pitchi Wuhl Wuhl the hopping mouse, who had big eyes, long whiskers and a tail with a tuft of hair at the end. Pitchi could stand on two legs to walk. He could also gallop.

Sometimes at dusk and dawn, Rusty met Bilby the Rabbit-eared Bandicoot, who came scooting from a burrow under a clump of spinifex. Like Rusty, Bilby ate termites.

Early one morning, a noisy machine flew in over the rocky mountains and landed on the flat. It had an engine that screeched louder than a flock of parrots, making Rusty run and hide. Two geologists had come to survey the hill for minerals.

'Won't take us long,' said Ted. 'Just time to collect some rock samples.'

They set off with sampling bags and tools. Nothing moved on the hill. The animals were in hiding from the sun. The men spent the day collecting, then spread out sleeping bags and lit a fire to cook a meal.

Ted looked around. 'This place is dead! But suppose we did find minerals here. There'd be houses, shops, schools…'

'It's pretty good the way it is,' said Bill. 'Seems a shame to crush the rock for minerals to build more factories to crush more rock.'

'Call yourself a geologist?' said Ted. 'We're out here to help this country's progress, not to stop it all.'

On the hill while the men slept, soundless hordes scampered. The native cat hunted the bandicoot. The bandicoot chased the mice. The mice were looking for beetles and the beetles were after ants.

Rusty was out in the early morning before the sun was up. The big machine bird was still there. One man was still in his sleeping bag, while the other was moving around.

Rusty was curious. He ran across the flat and poked his nose into a sampling bag but there was nothing inside but rocks.

He moved closer to the wheel of the bird and peeped around it at the man. But the man had seen him and was looking his way. Rusty stood still, his tail fluffed up in fright. The man began to move closer, closer, until Rusty felt the footsteps vibrating in the sand. He could not decide which way to run.

Bill dropped on one knee and held out his hand. Rusty didn't run. He poked his quivering nose forward to investigate the hand, and found himself scooped up and held!

He did not bite or scratch. 'Run!' his instincts told him, but he could not move. He hissed a warning to the hand but it stayed gently but firmly around him.

Ted rose from his sleeping bag and knocked over the billy, which fell with a clatter. HISS! Steam rose from the hot stones. Bill relaxed his grip on Rusty and Rusty leaped for the ground. He was gone before Ted could see what Bill had been holding in his hand.

'Did you see that!' gasped Bill. 'I had a numbat in my hand.'

'A what?'

'A numbat. Banded anteater. Didn't you see the stripes? There are numbats in the forests of the west, but not here in the desert. And this was a rusty one. They haven't been seen for fifty years. If I could only get a photograph...'

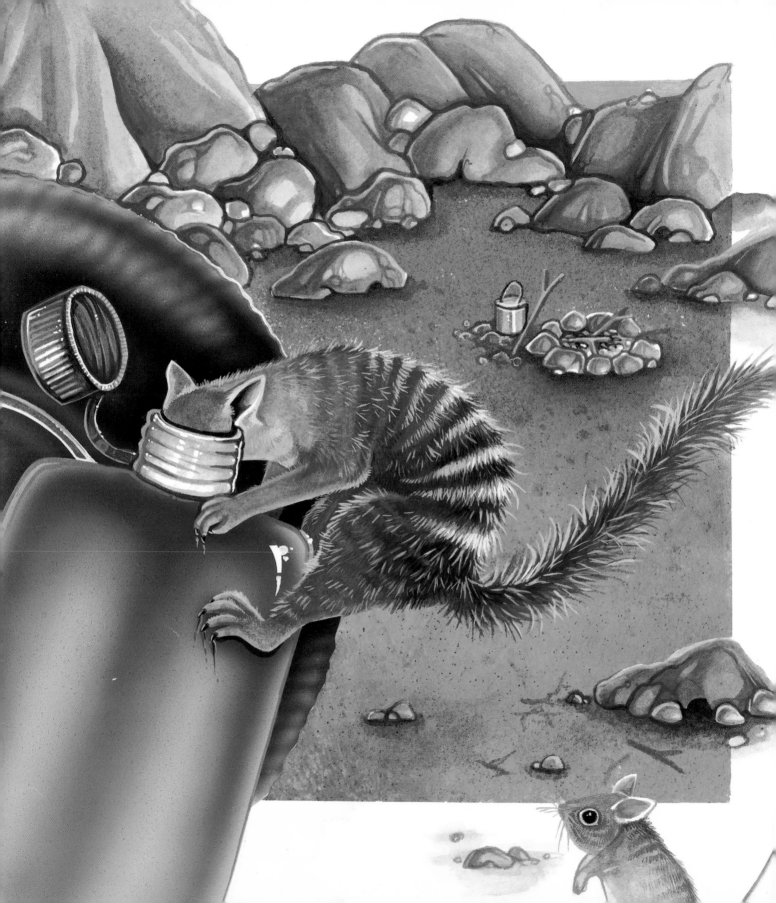

Ted was gathering up the bags. 'We're a day behind already.'

'But don't you realise?' said Bill. 'This is news!'

'News!' exploded Ted. 'Look Bill, I'm interested too. But the Company is waiting for our report. We can't sit here photographing animals, however rare.'

'But a rusty numbat is a treasure that can't be bought!'

'All right. We'll stay another day. I'll collect more samples and you can go looking for this numbat thing.'

Bill spent all day investigating holes, wondering which one might be Rusty's. At last he gave up and went back to writing his report, and sketching Rusty in between.

When the sun was going down and the air was becoming cool, Rusty came out of his hole, drawn once more to the camp. A water container stood underneath the giant bird, its lid almost off. Rusty poked his snout into the hole and kicked off from the ground. His head was stuck! He waved his feet in the air and the water bottle toppled sideways.

Bill dived to stop the bottle falling. Rusty was free, but water was pouring onto the thirsty ground. A damp patch spread under the plane.

'No one can stay here without water. We're taking off at the crack of dawn!' Ted declared.

But in the morning a dust storm came. The men spent the day sheltering in the plane. Food was no problem but they were very thirsty.

In the late afternoon, Rusty came scratching around the plane. Bill saw him and gave chase. Rusty ran up the slope and over the rocks, heading for one of his holes. At last he squeezed into a small space where he knew he would be safe.

But Bill was no longer watching him. He was bending down, cupping his hands together, scooping fresh spring water from a hole. He ran back to camp to get the container to replenish their water supply.

In the clear morning air the engine of the plane kicked into life. Ted and Bill were once again ready to leave, but first they boiled the billy for a quiet cup of tea.

'The city can wait,' said Ted. 'There are no useful minerals here. Your numbat friend will be safe for a while.'

As the plane flew away, Bill looked back at the hill, hoping to get a last glimpse of Rusty, but nothing moved under the sun.

'Borrow your pencil?' he asked. On the spot where they had landed he printed: NUMBAT RIDGE.

Numbats are found in some areas of Western Australia and South Australia, but the Rusty Numbat has not been seen for 50 years and may be extinct.